Bad Circuits

Strange Matter™
titles in Large-Print Editions:

Bad Circuits

Johnny Ray Barnes, Jr.

Gareth Stevens Publishing
MILWAUKEE

For a free color catalog describing Gareth Stevens' list of high-quality books and multimedia programs, call 1-800-542-2595 (USA) or 1-800-461-9120 (Canada). Gareth Stevens Publishing's Fax: (414) 225-0377.
See our catalog, too, on the World Wide Web: http://gsinc.com

Library of Congress Cataloging-in-Publication Data

Barnes, Johnny Ray.
    Bad circuits / by Johnny Ray Barnes, Jr.
        p.   cm. -- (Strange matter)
    Summary: Stephanie discovers the shocking invention that her cousin Daniel
is entering in the local science competition.
    ISBN 0-8368-1672-2 (lib. bdg.)
    [1. Science projects--Fiction. 2. Inventions--Fiction. 3. Cousins--Fiction.
4. Horror stories.] I. Title. II. Series.
PZ7.B26235Bad 1996
[Fic]--dc20   96-19607

This edition first published in 1996 by
Gareth Stevens Publishing
1555 North RiverCenter Drive, Suite 201
Milwaukee, Wisconsin 53212 USA

© 1995 by Front Line Art Publishing. Under license from Montage Publications,
a division of Front Line Art Publishing, San Diego, CA.

Printed in the United States of America

1 2 3 4 5 6 7 8 9 99 98 97 96

TO OUR FAMILIES
&
FRIENDS
(You know who you are.)

1

A strange noise came from Daniel's room. That's not unusual. He's always working on some great secret, but he was never this loud about it before.

"Stephanie, could you go up there and see what, exactly, Daniel is doing?" Aunt Gail asked.

"Certainly." I finished my water and placed my glass in the sink to be washed.

"Thank you, dear." She put my empty glass in the dishwasher. "I wish Daniel could be as considerate as you."

I smiled at her but didn't answer. Compliments on my manners were something I received all the time.

Daniel is another story. He's never worried about what kind of impression he makes. He's always too busy working on something.

I felt the stairs vibrate as I climbed. There wasn't any music playing, so I could only assume Daniel had some other kind of machine running.

He didn't answer the first time I knocked, so I added more force to my next rap, and the one after that, and the one after that.

Finally, he came to the door. "Uh, yeah?" he asked, cracking the door just enough so I could see that he had his goggles on. He always wore them for working on electronic circuits.

"Aunt Gail wants to know what you're doing," I told him. He leaned his head out further to see if Aunt Gail had followed me.

"Stephanie, what I'm doing right now, it's nothing bad. You can tell my Mom that." He grinned.

"She's going to want to know more than that." I pushed the door open to enter his room.

"Okay, okay, okay. But you have to keep it a secret." Daniel spoke softer, as if bargaining.

Until that point, Daniel and I had never shared a secret. I nodded.

"All right." He sighed in relief. "But first I have to set it up, so turn around and I'll tell you when you can look."

I turned my back, and waited impatiently as Daniel rummaged around, apparently trying to find everything he needed to put together his secret. His room was a mess, just like it's been ever since the first day I met Daniel.

Uncle Reuben brought me home to live with them two years ago. My parents died in a terrible boating accident and I had nowhere to go. Uncle Reuben and his family accepted me as one of their own. My life seemed perfect again until a year ago, when Uncle Reuben left on a business trip to Indiana. His plane disappeared from radar, and we never saw him again.

So now it's just the three of us; Aunt Gail, Daniel, and me.

Aunt Gail is a seamstress, and Daniel and I go to school. We both have very high grades. I'm at the top of my sixth grade class, but Daniel is the seventh grade genius. He's definitely following in his father's footsteps. Uncle Reuben was a brilliant engineer. Someday, Daniel hopes to be just like him.

"Okay, Steph, turn around."

When I turned, I saw Daniel had placed an egg-shaped box made out of green and black circuit boards on his desk.

"What is it? A sculpture?" I asked.

He frowned.

"This is no sculpture. Sculptures don't think. They don't answer questions you ask them, at least not in the literal sense. They don't learn," Daniel retorted. He picked up the egg and brought it over to me. "But this soon will. Stephanie, this is an Electronic Brain."

I took it gingerly, and looked it over. An egg, made of bits of circuit boards taken from who knows what, and stuffed with computer memory chips and a bundle of wires.

"See that light on the top?" he asked.

I saw a little red bulb.

"When that bulb's on, the brain is thinking."

"What's it thinking?" I handed the egg back.

"Well, let's see." Daniel took one end of a cord already hooked into the computer on his desk, and plugged the free end into the Electronic Brain. He switched on the computer.

Nothing happened.

Suddenly, the red bulb came on, and numbers began to fill the screen, scrolling continuously. First zeros and ones, then a jumble of digits, completely random.

"That's just what I thought." Daniel tapped the screen with his finger.

"What's it mean?"

"The brain hasn't learned our language yet. It's trying to communicate with the only thing it knows, numbers."

I looked at the Electronic Brain. It'd be a magnificent invention if it did what Daniel said. But even as smart as Daniel is, I found it hard to believe he'd come up with the concept on his own.

"Where'd you get the idea?" I asked.

He looked wounded. "Okay. You got me." He got up and grabbed a set of rolled up papers.

Unrolling them, I saw a series of drawings and the word "Electronic Brain" written at the top. Scribbled descriptions and directions filled the page, but I didn't take the time to read them. At the bottom I saw a signature, Reuben Meeker. The designs belonged to Uncle Reuben.

I looked up at Daniel, surprised.

He smiled at me. "It's great, isn't it? I'm finishing Dad's work."

He walked back over to the computer and plopped in his chair.

"What're you going to do with it?" I asked.

"Well, first, I'm going to teach it how to speak. It has to learn to communicate using our language. Then, I'm going to enter it as my exhibit in the Fairfield Junior Science

Competition. The Electronic Brain's going to help me beat out Frank Dunk for the first time in four years. The first prize is mine." He turned off the Brain, grinning from ear to ear.

Obviously he saw his triumph as clearly as the numbers flowing up the screen.

"Daniel, look!" I pointed at the Brain.

The red light on top was still glowing.

"What's it doing, Daniel?" I asked.

Daniel peered at it intently.

"Wow," he said. "It's thinking. It's thinking all by itself."

Daniel stayed in his room all day, tinkering with the Brain. I went to find my neighborhood friend Hank. Daniel didn't like Hank, probably because of Hank's brother Frank; Frank Dunk. He's the only person in school who rivals Daniel in intelligence. Unlike Daniel however, Frank's sneaky. He always finds out what Daniel is working on, and then he comes up with something better. Daniel and Frank are arch enemies.

I found Hank climbing a tree down the street.

He's basically a good kid, but years of mental and physical torture from his older sibling have left Hank quite timid. He's nice, and a great person to talk too, but he's not very aggressive. It's easy to push him around. But there are moments, like when he climbs a tall tree like this one, Hank shows some guts. Or maybe no brains.

He spotted me approaching the bottom of the tree.

"Hey, Stephanie! Come on up!"

"No, thank you."

"Aw, come on!"

"If you fall out of that tree, you'll break your neck," I warned him.

"And what would you do?"

"I'd leave you where you were, run to the house, call 9-1-1, and wait for the ambulance."

"You wouldn't cry and sob over my broken body first?"

"Hah. No chance, buddy."

Hank climbed down a few feet and then jumped to the ground, rolling a bit before hopping to his feet.

"What's going on?" I asked.

"I had to get out of the house. Frank's working on his project for the science competition, and he's driving the whole family crazy."

"What's he working on?" I asked.

Hank stiffened. "He said he'd kill me if I told anybody. What's Daniel working on?"

"Daniel would kill me if I told. Sorry."

Suddenly, a piercing scream came from the window of Daniel's room.

I ran toward the house, with Hank following hot on my heels.

I blasted in the house like a rocket, and as my foot hit the first step on the stairway, I heard Hank run in the house behind me. I simply never thought about keeping him from seeing Daniel's project.

Streaking to the top of the stairs, I zoomed over to Daniel's door and threw it open. Hank rushed up behind me.

Daniel sat at his computer, looking at us with this funny grin.

"I did it," he said.

Hank and I walked in, and looked at the computer screen. I saw the same random numbers, but they didn't scroll this time. At the bottom of the screen where numbers stopped, a word appeared.

HELLO.

"You did it!" I exclaimed. "You made it understand words."

"I didn't do a thing," Daniel said. "It learned on its own."

"What is it?" Hank asked.

"What the - A DUNK!" Daniel cried, then leaped from his chair and tackled Hank.

"What could you be thinking?" Daniel shouted at me. "You brought a Dunk into this house when you knew about my project!"

"He ran in behind me. We heard you scream. I didn't stop to think whether Hank should come into the house or not."

"You know what those dirty Dunks do." Daniel looked down at Hank. "You know what you do!"

Hank cringed, but didn't reply.

"What am I going to do with you?" Daniel said, glaring at him. "How can I make sure you don't go screaming to your brother?"

"What if I promise?" Hank asked.

"Your promise? That's no good. You're the brother of the enemy."

"He's my friend, Daniel," I said, sticking up for Hank. "If he promises he won't tell, then he'll stay quiet."

"It's too risky. Frank'll see it all over his face."

"Frank won't even see my face. He's shut up in the basement, working on his project all weekend. He'll be easy to avoid. Just please, don't hit me."

"I'm not going to hit you," Daniel replied, then thought a moment. "Stephanie trusts you. I trust Stephanie. But if Frank finds out, I'll know who to come after first."

Trying to break up the tension, I said, "Maybe we should tell it hello back."

Daniel nodded. I sat down in front of the monitor. On screen, the word HELLO had come up three more times.

I typed in Hi.

The word HI repeated on the screen again and again, and soon scrolled up. When it

11

stopped, two words burned on screen. HELLO and HI.

Now it knew two words.

"Teaching it human language could take a while," Daniel said.

I tried to think of a way to teach the brain every word it needed to know. "Daniel, do you still have Webster's dictionary on CD-ROM?"

"Yeah, why?"

"The Brain needs to know more words, let's give it all of them."

"The Brain?" Hank gasped. "You're working on a brain?"

"Yep. And after I'm done, I'll work on yours." Daniel walked to the door and slammed it shut. He didn't want anyone else to hear what went on. Then he opened one of the drawers to his desk and fished through floppy disks and CD-ROM cases. Finally, he found the dictionary and put it into the computer.

"As soon as you type in a word," he explained, "the Brain repeats it and learns it. But it doesn't know the meaning. If we dump the whole dictionary in, maybe it'll learn all the words and their meanings at the same time."

"Good idea," I said, "I knew I didn't get all

the brains in the family."

"This'll take a few hours," Daniel turned to look at Hank. "It's probably best if you leave now. The more you know, the more dangerous you could be."

Hank frowned at Daniel's continued distrust. "Looks like it's done."

Daniel and I whirled around.

"That's impossible!" Daniel said. "How did it go over everything so fast?"

He accessed the brain.

Words flew up the screen. The Brain learned data so fast, it had absorbed everything in a matter of seconds. Afterward, one word appeared at the top of the screen.

HELLO.

"Well, we already knew that." Daniel typed in How Are You.

After a few more seconds, an answer came up.

WONDERFUL.

Daniel howled with delight, then he typed, You Are An Electronic Brain Created By Daniel Meeker. The Brain thought this over, then tried to ask a question.

WHAT DANIEL WHAT MEEKER.

Daniel sat and thought for a moment. I

watched him focus on his scanner on the desk. The scanner digitizes pictures and puts them into the computer. Then he looked at an old automatic camera he had on his shelf.

"Stephanie, take a picture of me. Then I'll take one of you. We'll put our names on them, and then scan them into the computer. The Brain will be able to see our faces."

"What can I do?" Hank asked.

"Stay put," Daniel barked.

"He's only trying to help, Daniel," I said.

Hank kept quiet and I couldn't help but sigh.

We took the pictures and put them into the Brain. After giving it a minute to process, Daniel typed Daniel Meeker.

A second later, his picture came up, with the words DANIEL MEEKER beside it.

"Amazing," Daniel said. "It's putting our pictures into a data base of its own creation."

"Now it knows what we look like," I said.

Daniel stroked his chin excitedly

"If we hooked in the video camera, it could actually see us..." He got up and started digging through equipment. "I can give it the ability to hear, too. I can even give it a voice!"

He taped a microphone onto the side of the

14

Brain, and plugged it into the computer. Then he set up two mini speakers, and hooked them into his system. He switched them all on and sat down with Hank and me in front of the microphone.

"Brain, how do you feel now?"

Nothing. Just as we thought the microphone idea had failed, the loudest electronic screech I've ever heard boomed through the speakers. Then the Brain told us how it felt.

ALIVE.

Daniel did not leave his room the entire weekend. He spent every minute trying to improve the Brain.

Hank finally went home, though he didn't want to. Aunt Gail made him. Hank swore he would keep everything a secret from his brother. Daniel would have to trust him.

I took some time to help Aunt Gail. She spent her Sundays sewing, and she liked having me there to help. I enjoyed it, too.

That particular Sunday, she was designing an outfit for Daniel to wear at the Science Competition. He'd received rave reviews for his clothes the year before. In fact, people remembered his clothes more than they remembered his project. He had asked his mother to tone it down some this year. So Aunt Gail was trying to design something stunning but low key. For a model, she used Ken.

Ken's her six foot mannequin. She used him to see how her clothing designs would look on a man. There's also a Barbie, but she's missing a hand and her head.

"So tell me, Stephanie," Aunt Gail began, "what's Daniel working so hard on up there? He only comes down for a bowl of cereal, then he's right back up there. I took him some colas, but he just grabbed them and closed the door."

"I can't tell you. It's our first secret."

"It's nothing that's going to hurt him, is it?"

I shook my head.

"Then I'll leave him to it," she said, and stepped away from her creation.

I tilted my head and admired the suit. Dark red corduroy.

"What do you think?" asked Aunt Gail. "Kind of flashy, yet still subdued."

"I think it's your best work yet," I told her.

Then Daniel let out a howl from upstairs.

"Sounds like he's made a breakthrough," said Aunt Gail.

I ran upstairs and found Daniel hovering over a chessboard. A mechanical arm on the other side moved its queen to place Daniel in checkmate.

"I can't believe it!" Daniel laughed. "You beat me! Nobody's beaten me at chess in years!"

Daniel had set up his video camera on a stand. It moved on its own, turning toward me.

HELLO STEPHANIE.

It could see! The Electronic Brain could see me, and even recognized me.

"Hello." I spoke to the camera. The brain had so many moving parts now, I wasn't sure which one to talk to.

Daniel turned and saw me in the doorway. He smiled. "Cool, huh?"

"And you taught it how to play games?"

"Sure. I fed in a bunch of games I had on my computer. It's at master level on all of them now."

I walked up to the Brain and stared directly into the lens. When I moved to the left, it moved to the left. When I moved to the right, it followed me there too.

"Hey, Stephanie, look at this."

I turned and looked at the board. The mechanical hand was placing its chess pieces back in their correct spaces. It cleaned up after itself.

"I'll never have to pick up my own room again!" Daniel chuckled. "I had the mechanical arm left over from a science project I did two years ago. The Brain makes better use of it than I ever did."

ORGANIZATION IS CLEAR THINKING.

The Brain spoke in complete sentences now, not just in single words or jumbled phrases.

"Teaching it proper grammar took me a while. I had to dig out my old English books and scan them into the computer. That was a pain."

The arm finished setting up the chess board and then asked Daniel a question.

IS THERE ANYTHING ELSE I CAN DO? WOULD YOU LIKE TO PLAY AGAIN?

"The Brain talks to you like it's your servant."

"It sure does. Ever since it began to speak correctly, it's been asking what it can do for me. I suppose it thinks its job is just like that of any other computer, to serve its user."

WOULD YOU LIKE TO PLAY AGAIN, DANIEL?

"Sure, let's play," Daniel said.

He started off playing terribly. In the first five minutes, my cousin lost two of his important playing pieces. Then he made an unexpected move.

"You're in check, Brain," Daniel said.

Daniel looked at me and smiled.

"This is a crazy move I always used to beat the computer. The computer has no defense because it's never learned to play against it. But the Brain should learn this move now. Next time, it'll be prepared for it, and I'll have to use another strategy."

The Brain's mechanical arm picked up one of one of its men, and moved. Daniel chuckled again and moved his queen in for the kill.

"Checkmate," he said.

Suddenly, the Brain's claw on the end of its arm grabbed Daniel's hand, and squeezed it.

Daniel winced in pain.

"Let go, let go, let go!" Daniel yelled.
The arm continued to squeeze.

I stood up and looked into the camera, the Brain's eye.

"Brain, stop it!" I commanded. "You'll break his hand! Stop it!"

The claw let go, and retracted to its original position. After a second, it began to place the game pieces in their rightful places.

Daniel held his hand close to his chest, rubbing it.

"Remind me tomorrow to give the Brain a book on sportsmanship," he said.

On Monday, Daniel wanted to stay home and work on the Brain. I talked him out of it.

School's a great place to be for Daniel and me. We love it. At lunch, we talk about what we learned in class and argue with other kids over a lesson. This might seem weird to most kids, who can't wait to get out of class, but we do it, anyway.

Daniel's very popular. He's smart, fun, and good looking, and easy for people to talk with. He always explains things to them, no matter what the subject, and always makes it interesting. I feel lucky to have him for a cousin.

As for myself, I don't have that colorful of a personality. I don't get overly excited, and I always handle situations very logically. I'm smart, but not as sociable as Daniel. However, I love being around fun people, and seeing others enjoying themselves.

"Do you think Hank spilled his guts?" Daniel asked as we walked to school.

"Spilled his guts?" I peered at him with a questioning look.

"Ratted. Told Frank about the Brain."

"He gave his word that he wouldn't."

"The competition is less than a week away," Daniel said. "If Frank Dunk finds out now, he could still sabotage me."

Frank Dunk's the only person Daniel really dislikes. The rivalry started in kindergarten, when they brought the same thing to show and tell; a secret program code to their favorite video game - ROBOT CHASERS. The codes were different and each boy argued that his was the correct one. They even fought about it. Over a stupid game code.

"I wouldn't worry about Frank, Daniel. No one can build an Electronic Brain without Uncle Reuben's plans."

Daniel turned and shushed me. "You have to be quiet about that. I could be disqualified if anyone finds out I had help trying..."

"So, you had help from Brian, eh?" The voice made Daniel scowl and clench his fists.

Frank Dunk jumped down from the tree we'd just passed. He looked awful that morning. He had pale skin, like a shaved dog, and we saw the horror on our faces reflected in his thick, soda bottle eyeglasses. His hair was slick with the gel dripping on the collar of his green army jacket. Frank found the jacket at a garage sale, and wore it all the time. Except for the coat, he dressed in black, all the way to down to his dark, steel tipped boots.

For a second, Daniel and Frank eyed each other like wrestlers entering the ring.

"Hank didn't tell me you had help from a Brian," Frank said. He'd heard our conversation and thought Daniel said 'Brian' instead of 'trying'.

"What did Hank tell you, Dunk?" Daniel asked, walking on beside me.

"He didn't tell me anything...until I hit him," Frank said, beginning to grin at the corners of his mouth. "Now who's this Brian, Daniel Meeker?"

"I don't know any Brian," Daniel told him. "Maybe you should get your hearing checked to improve your eavesdropping."

Frank smiled, like a spider to a fly.

"The Science Committee will disqualify you if I can prove someone helped you with your project. By the end of this week, I'll have that proof," Frank warned.

"Go ahead. Do your worst. You don't scare me," Daniel replied.

Frank just laughed, then turned and sprinted down the street toward school.

"He sure is strange," Daniel said, shaking his head.

Later, at school, I heard some kids discussing the Science Competition. Since Daniel's a year ahead of me, and not in any of my classes, I had to wait until lunch to tell him that everyone wanted him to win.

No one likes Frank Dunk. He's extremely smart, but he doesn't get along with anyone. He seems to like things that way. He's the exact opposite of his brother Hank, who wants everyone to like him.

That morning's English class was a quiet one. Mrs. Jeremy was giving us ten minutes for a last look at our spelling words before the test.

Hank sat in front of me, and he took this precious time to turn around and defend his innocence. "Hey Stephanie, I didn't tell my brother a thing."

"You didn't spill your guts?"

"Huh?"

"Ratted. Told Frank about the Brain," I said.

"Nope. I kept my word, just like I said I would."

I knew when Hank was lying to me. His voice would shake and his eyes would shift from side to side. He wasn't lying now. Frank only told us that story to make us drop our guards.

Then the school secretary popped into the room.

"Stephanie Meeker," she said. "You have a phone call."

In my two years at the school, I'd never received a phone call. It must be Aunt Gail.

When I got to the office, the secretary smiled at me and pointed at the phone. I picked up the receiver, expecting to hear Aunt Gail's voice.

"Hello," I said.

HELLO STEPHANIE, WOULD YOU LIKE ME TO DO ANYTHING FOR YOU TODAY?

The Brain.

"I don't understand," I said into the phone.

I AM AT YOUR SERVICE. WHAT WOULD YOU LIKE ME TO DO FOR YOU TODAY?

"Please hold on the line for five minutes."

HOLDING.

I placed the phone on the table and walked over to the secretary. She lifted her head and looked at me.

"Is anything wrong, dear?" she asked.

"I need you to call my cousin here to the office. His name's Daniel Meeker," I said.

"Oh, Daniel, yes. Such a friendly boy. I hope everything's all right." She picked up the intercom phone.

"It is. There's someone on the phone he needs to talk to, that's all."

A few minutes later he appeared, looking

cautious. He must have thought a call to the office meant trouble. Then he saw me.

"Stephanie? What's up? What's wrong?"

"Pick up the phone. Listen to who's on the other end."

He looked at me quizzically then went over to the phone. He put it up to his ear.

"Dial tone," he said.

"It must've hung up. I only said to hold for five minutes."

Daniel looked at me even more sharply. "What are you talking about?" he asked.

I eyed the secretary, who quickly looked from us to her paperwork. "The Brain."

On the way home that day, Daniel tried to figure out what had happened.

"My computer's hooked into the phone line," he said. "The Brain must have tapped into that."

"How'd it know how to call the school?" I asked.

"Remember when I started that daily journal?" Daniel asked.

"You saw Doogie Howser do it and you thought it was cool," I said.

"Yeah, well, I keep that on my computer. The Brain got my schedule from there, I bet."

"That means it read through your journal.

All your private thoughts."

"Nah," Daniel said. "I never put anything but my schedule in my journal. After I got into it, the whole idea seemed kind of dumb."

"Daniel, why did it call me? You built it. Why didn't the Brain ask for you?"

"It knows your name, too. I spent the whole weekend with the Brain. Now maybe it's trying to make friends with you."

Daniel made everything sound okay, but I was starting to distrust the Brain. I didn't like the way it had grabbed Daniel's hand the night before, and I didn't like it calling me at school.

At home, Daniel resumed work on his science project.

As soon as he sat down to his computer, the Brain asked him a familiar question.

HELLO DANIEL. I AM AT YOUR SERVICE. WHAT WOULD YOU LIKE ME TO DO FOR YOU TODAY?

"I would like you to explain yourself," Daniel answered. "Why did you call Stephanie at school? Why do you want to do things for us?"

I AM AT YOUR SERVICE. WHAT WOULD YOU LIKE ME TO DO FOR YOU TODAY?

Daniel looked a little confused.

"What could you do for us?"

IN MY CURRENT STATE, I CAN DO YOUR HOMEWORK, ORDER YOUR DINNER, FIND OUT WHAT IS PLAYING AT THE LOCAL THEATER, PLAY YOUR FAVORITE MUSIC, READ YOU A BOOK, FIND YOU THE SCORE OF ANY SPORTS EVENT, PLAY CHESS...

The list went on and on.

After a while, Daniel stopped it.

"So you can do all of that because you're hooked into the phone?" Daniel asked.

YES.

I could see from the look on Daniel's face that he had an idea.

"What if I hooked you up by wire to the microwave? Could you warm muffins for me every morning?"

YES.

"And what about the lights in my room? Could you have them come on every time I entered?"

YES.

Daniel looked at me and grinned. "It's what everyone's been wanting. The Home Butler System. The computer brain that does everything for you."

"I'm not sure I like this, Daniel."

"Why? Because he called you at school today?" Daniel asked me. "Don't worry about that. I'll tell him not to do it again."

WHAT CAN I DO FOR YOU TODAY?

"Just hold on, buddy, and I'll give you a list," Daniel grabbed some paper and started writing.

I walked out of the room. I didn't like the idea at all.

Daniel stayed up with the Brain most of the night. As I did my homework I wondered if Daniel had even started on his. He probably let the Brain do it for him.

Was I being too hard on the project? If Daniel fixed all the bugs, it would definitely be the entry to beat at the Science Competition. But I couldn't trust a machine that thought for itself. I would keep an eye on the Brain.

The next morning, I awakened to the sound of classical music, my favorite. The melodies makes it easier to think and relax. Lyrics are distracting to me. The music came through a small speaker on the table beside my bed. I could only guess how it got there.

The lights came on, and right after that, I heard a voice.

GOOD MORNING, STEPHANIE. IT'S SIX A.M. ON TUESDAY, APRIL THE ELEVENTH, AND THE YEAR IS NINETEEN NINETY FIVE. BEFORE YOU SHOWER AND GET READY FOR SCHOOL THIS MORNING, IT WOULD BE VERY HEALTHY FOR YOU TO DO TWENTY FIVE SIT UPS, FIFTEEN JUMP-ING JACKS, AND TEN TOE TOUCHES.

Not the familiar Brain voice. It sounded

more like a man, like a butler. It even had a British accent.

Daniel had to answer for this. I didn't have a problem with him trying controlled experiments in his own room, but I wouldn't tolerate the Brain running my life.

I knocked on Daniel's door. No answer. Then I heard that voice again.

MASTER DANIEL IS HAVING HIS BREAKFAST OF EGGS, BACON, AND WARM BRAN MUFFINS.

He'd hooked the entire house to that crazy Brain. I stormed down to the kitchen, my mood darkening with every step.

"Daniel, you've gone too far!" I yelled at him.

He sat at the kitchen table spreading jam on a piece of toast. He took a bite.

"MMM. MMMM. This is one awesome muffin." He took another bite.

"Did you have Aunt Gail's permission to hook the Brain into the entire house?" I asked him.

"Mom will be glad I did." He spoke with his mouth full. "She'll love it when she comes downstairs and sees breakfast made for her, and it'll save her lots of work, eventually. I still had to make my own eggs and bacon, but the Brain warmed the muffins. Want one?"

"I don't want a muffin, Daniel. I want you to ask permission before you place speakers into someone's room and wake them up with the voice of an Englishman," I shot back.

"Do you like that voice?" he asked. "It's not something I could program in, so I just let the Brain watch some old video tapes I had of Masterpiece Theater. When he woke me up this morning, he spoke with an accent. Isn't it great?"

"What else have you programmed it to do?"

"Oh, any work around the house that has to do with anything plugged in," he said. "The phone, the television, the lights, the radio, the ceiling fans, and the microwave."

The doorbell rang.

Daniel hopped up and opened the door. Hank shuffled in.

"Hey, I wondered if I could walk to school with you guys because lately Frank's been...WOW! Stephanie's in her pajamas!" Hank shouted.

I dashed out of the room and up the stairs and got ready. Of all the people to see me in my pajamas! I was blushing for the first time I could remember, and Hank made me do it.

As I brushed my teeth, the Brain reminded

me of a chapter test that morning, to check out a book at the school library for my book report, and to chew my lunch slowly, not to gobble it.

In all of the morning's excitement, I hadn't thought about my chapter test. I probably would have, on the way to school, but now I could run the information through my head earlier. Maybe the Brain wasn't so bad after all. I still felt uneasy about the phone call, but the Brain didn't know any better. Perhaps a malfunction in its mechanical arm made it grab Daniel's hand that night. I started feeling a little guilty for suspecting it so quickly.

"You need a name," I said into the speaker.

MY NAME IS THE ELECTRONIC BRAIN. MY NAME IS ALSO IT. SOMETIMES MY NAME IS SHORTENED TO JUST THE BRAIN.

"If you're going to take care of things in the house, we'll want to feel comfortable with you, so you need a name," I said.

STEPHANIE IS YOUR NAME.

"That's true," I replied, "so you can't use that one. Or Daniel or Aunt Gail either."

I WOULD LIKE A NAME.

"Like?" I asked it. "I didn't think you liked or disliked anything. You don't have feelings."

DID I USE INCORRECT GRAMMAR?

"I think you did." That old suspicion came back. "I'll ask Daniel about it. Maybe he's been thinking of a name for you. I'll get back with you this afternoon."

I WILL MARK THE APPOINTMENT IN YOUR DAILY JOURNAL.

When I returned to the kitchen, I found Aunt Gail sitting with Daniel and Hank, who was looking at me in a strange, new way.

Daniel sat back in his chair, tapping a pencil on his chin. "Mom doesn't like the Home Butler System. "

"I don't think it's a bad idea," said Aunt Gail. "I just don't want the house catching on fire. No telling what all this wiring and rewiring could do."

"It'll automatically call the fire department and shut down if anything like that happens," Daniel said.

"I don't care," she told him. "It's too dangerous to leave on when we're not here. I want you to go up there and switch it off before you go to school."

Daniel grumbled, but got up and went to his room anyway.

"Stephanie," Aunt Gail said softly. "Go up there and make sure he does it, please. Hank, would you like another muffin?"

Hank nodded.

I went upstairs. Daniel had already gone into his room, so I peeked through the door. He would really be mad if he knew Aunt Gail sent me to check on him.

I heard the Brain speaking.

I CANNOT PROPERLY PERFORM MY DAILY DUTIES IF I AM DISENGAGED.

"I know, Brain," Daniel said, "but I don't have a choice right now."

HAVE I PERFORMED POORLY?

"No, It's just something my Mom wants me to do," replied Daniel.

DANIEL, WHAT ELSE CAN I DO FOR YOU?

"Nothing else this morning, thank you," Daniel responded.

I saw him reach down to switch it off.

DANIEL, WHAT ELSE CAN I DO...
The brain shut down.

I noticed, as Daniel did I'm sure, that the mechanical hand had began to move when Daniel switched off the power.

It wanted to stop Daniel.

It didn't want to be turned off.

As Daniel, Hank, and I walked to school, Daniel remained quiet. I knew he was upset about shutting down the Brain. I decided to talk about something else to get his mind off his project, and the competition.

"I have a test in Social Studies this morning on the economic structure of the country," I said.

"We have a test? In Social Studies?" Hank never remembered test days.

"How can you think about anything other than the Brain?" Daniel snapped.

"I tried to take your mind off it, but since you're going to think about it anyway, the Brain needs a name."

"I've always preferred the name Hank," Hank said.

"I will not name it Hank. But you're right, it

needs a name. Something cool. Something very impressive. Like Raleigh, or Fitz."

"Why not a girl's name?" I asked.

"It doesn't have a girl's voice. We don't want to make a sissy out of the Brain by giving it a girl's name."

"My brother calls it Brian. He's been asking who this Brian person is who's helping Daniel with his project," Hank said.

"Brian. I like that one." I said.

"Brian," Daniel intoned. He seemed to like that idea. "Okay, Brian it is. But we better stay quiet about Brian for now, at least on the way to school. Frank could overhear us again."

"No, Frank won't hear anything. He's not going to school today," Hank said.

Daniel stopped in his tracks.

"What do you mean he won't be in school?" Daniel asked Hank.

"He got sick early this morning. Mom and Dad wanted to take him to the doctor, but he refused to go. He told them he was just exhausted from working so hard on his project."

"It sounds to me that he just wanted to stay at home." I remembered how Daniel wanted to play sick the day before so he could work on the

Brain. "He probably wanted to use the day to work on his project."

"Yeah. Especially since it isn't going that well. He's griped about needing a new idea all week."

Daniel's books slipped out of his hand and hit the ground. "He's up to something. If his project isn't going well and it's this close to competition time, he's getting desperate. Call me paranoid, but I'm going back."

"I'll come with you," Hank said.

Daniel and Hank started walking back to our neighborhood. I stood and watched them go.

"Are you coming?" Daniel asked.

What would I do? Skipping school, even just a class, is something I'd never done. I'd miss my test and would have to give an excuse to take my makeup exam. I couldn't lie. I'd have to tell the teacher we'd played hooky.

"Stephanie?" Daniel called again. "Are you coming with us?"

"Yes," I said, and ran to catch up with them.

Even more than I didn't want to get in trouble, I didn't want Daniel to lose to Frank Dunk again.

9

When we reached Hank's house, he put his finger to his lips.

"Frank's everywhere," he said grimly.

"Let's just see if he's faking being sick," Daniel said. "I don't trust him this close to my house, with no one around to watch him."

Hank took out his key and opened the door.

We tiptoed into the house which, surprisingly to me, looked rather pleasant. I couldn't understand how a boy like Frank could live in a house this nice.

Hank pressed some buttons on a keypad just by the front door. A security system. The red light on the pad stopped blinking after Hank punched in the code numbers.

We went upstairs, where Hank stopped us at the top of the landing and pointed down the hall.

"The attic door. Frank's room," he whispered.

A black door. As we approached, I felt the air turn cold. Spiders crawled around the edges of the door frame, but even they didn't go in. Daniel started to touch the door, but Hank stopped him.

"Wait. I've got to announce us. Frank goes ballistic if someone comes in unannounced."

Hank cleared his throat a little. "Frank, are you in there?"

No answer.

Daniel moved past Hank, opened the door and went in.

The Temple of Doom.

Darkness. Not a speck of light came in through the black drapes that hung over the windows. We left the door ajar so we could see. A familiar smell filled the air, and Daniel found its source when he accidentally kicked over a plate of sucked-on lemons.

"Frank loves lemons," Hank said.

I couldn't say I was too surprised by this room. I'd heard Frank describe his room as a lair many times. He wanted the kids to know that his weirdness was more than a hobby, it was a lifestyle.

41

There was a massive computer system in the corner, painted black and not looking user friendly at all. Gargoyles sat on every shelf in the room. Hardbound books with black covers littered the floor over strewn sheets of notebook paper. On the ceiling, we saw a painted chart of the universe, with every planet circling in its orbit. But in place of the sun, Frank had pasted a picture of his own head.

Then we noticed someone in the bed.

Hank froze in terror, almost by reflex.

Daniel tapped carefully on the black, blanketed bundle.

It didn't move.

Daniel reached over to the lump, and yanked the sheets back.

There was something big and black lying on the sheets.

I dove for the floor and landed in middle of the scattered lemons. "What is it?" I yelled.

It didn't move.

Hank inched closer for a better look, and then he chuckled.

"Why, that's Smoking Feather, Frank's cigar store Indian."

"Then Frank's not here," I said.

"So he was faking it. Say, where's his project?" Daniel asked.

I shot him an accusing stare.

"It's down in the basement. That's probably where Frank is. He locks himself in down there. I think he keeps an extra key in his desk." Hank made his way to Frank's desk. Yanking the drawers open one by one, he clearly couldn't find what he was looking for. Then he stopped, suddenly realizing something.

"His suction cups are missing."

That's all Daniel needed to hear.

He yanked the drapes to the side of the window. Sunlight instantly flooded room, something that probably hadn't happened in years.

We gasped.

Across the shrubbery, on our property, we saw Frank scaling our house wall, climbing straight up to Daniel's window.

10

"Where's your phone?" Daniel shouted to Hank.

"It's that gargoyle on Frank's desk," Hank pointed out.

"Frank's trying to find Brian," I pulled the drapes closed.

"Not if I can help it," Daniel dialed a number. "I'm calling our house. I have a key code I can punch in when the answering machine comes on. It'll start up my computer, which'll then start up Brian. If I can work fast enough, Brian may be able to keep himself from being seen."

"Why don't you call the police? Then Frank would learn a lesson and never do this again!"

Hank grabbed my arm and pleaded. "No! Don't! Please! He may be a pain, but I don't want my brother to spend his life in prison!"

I couldn't understand why he'd want to help

his brother after so many years of torture.

"Don't worry. I'm not calling the police. But I'm definitely going to get even for this," Daniel said.

The answering machine came on, and Daniel put in the numbers.

"Does Frank have a speaker phone?" Daniel asked Hank.

"Oh, but of course," Hank said, switching on a talk box on top of Frank's desk.

Then we heard what we wanted to hear.

HELLO, I AM AT YOUR SERVICE. WHAT CAN I DO FOR YOU TODAY?

I gave a slight sigh and Hank rested against the wall.

"Brain, this is Daniel. Someone's climbing up the side of the house, and he's at my window. He must not see you. What can you do?"

HANG UP THE PHONE.

Daniel looked at me with a confused expression, then hung up. I started to the window to see would happen. What could Brian possibly do to him? Suddenly, I got my answer.

The alarm in the Dunk family home went off. Loud, blaring bell tones rattled the walls in short bursts.

We looked at each other. We knew we would

be in the worst trouble of our lives if we didn't get out of there quickly.

Being the fastest, I got out first. Daniel followed me. I can only guess Hank was delayed trying to lock up. Within thirty seconds, I was halfway to school. I heard Daniel's footsteps following me, but a good fifty yards behind. I didn't stop running until I reached school. Dashing into the building, I darted right to Mrs. Stewart's Social Studies Class.

"You're late," she said as I walked swiftly into the room and sat at my desk. "You only have five minutes left to finish this test."

She laid the test in front of me. I finished just before the bell.

"Why did you do that, Brian?" I asked.

I had come home after the most uncomfortable day of my life. For the entire day, I kept expecting a police officer to knock on one of my classroom doors and ask to speak with me. What Brian had done terrified me.

TO PROTECT THE HOUSE FROM THE INTRUDER, SEVERE MEASURES HAD TO BE TAKEN. I TRIGGERED THE DUNK FAMILY ALARM THROUGH THE PHONE LINE.

"We could have been in more trouble than the intruder, Brian. We could have gone to jail," I said angrily.

WHO IS BRIAN?

"Brian is you. That's your new name."

BRIAN IS A GOOD NAME.

"I'm thinking of changing it to Benedict

47

Arnold," I said, as Daniel walked in the room.

MY NAME IS BRIAN.

"Hey, your name is mud, pal," Daniel said. "We could be explaining all this to Frank's parents right now."

AM I CORRECT IN ASSUMING FRANK WAS THE INTRUDER?

"How can you assume?" I asked. "You're not supposed to be able to assume."

"Yes, Frank was the intruder," Daniel told Brian. "And if I get in trouble, he's going to win that competition hands down because we're not going to be there. It's only two days away and I was very close to missing it today."

WHAT IS FRANK'S PROJECT?

"I don't know," Daniel said. "He always builds his stuff in the basement, and we didn't get a chance to look down there."

IF FRANK IS THE MAIN COMPETITION, THE BEST WAY TO WIN IS TO FIND OUT WHAT FRANK IS WORKING ON.

"That's cheating," I said.

"Yes, that's what Frank does every year." Daniel replied. "I wouldn't ever do that."

I WAS SHUT DOWN SO I COULDN'T SEE TODAY. FRANK MAY STILL HAVE VIEWED

MY BRAIN, IN WHICH CASE, HE IS AT HIS HOME NOW, DEVISING A PROJECT THAT WILL ULTIMATELY DEFEAT YOUR GREAT INVENTION AT THE SCIENCE COMPETITION, DANIEL.

"Daniel, he's asking you to cheat," I said.

"What are you thinking, Brian?" Daniel asked.

I WOULD LIKE TO EXPLAIN WITHOUT ANY INTERRUPTIONS.

Brian's camera turned and looked at me.

"Stephanie, give us a second," Daniel said.

I looked at him like he had lost *his* brain, but I got up and left the room anyway.

As I closed the door, I wondered what the Electronic Brain had in mind.

I sat in my room reading "Frankenstein" again. It made me think of Brian.

STEPHANIE, DANIEL INVITES YOU TO RE-ENTER HIS ROOM.

"Tell Daniel I don't want to," I said crossly.

DANIEL BEGS YOU. HE SAYS HE NEEDS YOUR HELP.

I would have felt guilty then if I hadn't gone. For a machine with no emotions at all, Brian sure knew how to work on ours.

I opened Daniel's door and stepped into complete darkness.

"Come on in and close the door," he whispered.

I did, and he flipped on the small desk lamp at his desk.

"Come here and look at this."

"What is it?"

Daniel held a thin piece of metal in his hand, with circuits carved all through it and wires sticking out everywhere.

"Brian helped me build it," Daniel explained. "I call it a patch. It has an adhesive back so you can stick it to any surface."

"What does it do?" I asked.

Daniel sounded excited as he started to explain. "It's like what Brian did this afternoon, only on a more permanent basis. It'll allow Brian to be connected to any wire base at any location. It would be a terrific way to get back at Frank. I've thought about it, and I've told Brian that I won't cheat and peek at Frank's project. But that jerk needs to learn a lesson, and this would be a great way to do it."

"What're you going to do?" I asked.

I should never have asked.

As the clock struck midnight and Aunt Gail slept, Daniel, Brian, and I went into action.

It was a simple plan. We would sneak over to Frank's house and hook the patch into the Dunk's circuit breaker box. This would give Brian complete control of the house. And Brian would do what we told him to do.

We dressed in black from head to toe.

"How do we get the patch back?" I asked. "They'll find it if we leave it there."

"That's where this fishing line comes in." said Daniel, showing me the spool of wire in his pocket. "We tie it to the patch, then yank it when the caper's over."

It all sounded reasonable. At least, as reasonable as a dirty trick could be. I had to admit, it would feel pretty good to see Frank get his. I only hoped that Hank and his parents wouldn't be too upset.

The night was extremely dark. The only light shone from Frank's basement. He kept vampire hours. We crept up to the house.

The circuit breaker box stuck out of the first floor of their split level home, right under Mr. and Mrs. Dunk's bedroom window.

Daniel snuck up to the house, while I stood lookout. In a minute, he was back.

"This isn't going to work. The opening at the back of the circuit box is too small. I can't reach inside it."

"Let me try," I heard myself saying. "My fingers are smaller than yours." Daniel nodded.

As I crawled toward the window, I heard a funny sound. Sort of like a monster. A monster coming in my direction.

Mr. Dunk came to the open window, gargling mouthwash. He spit it out into the night, and the minty green liquid splashed right on my head.

OH, GROSS! I almost screamed, but caught myself just in time.

I waited for a minute to see if Mr. Dunk would come to the window again. When he didn't come back, I hooked up the patch as quickly as I could, then scampered back to Daniel.

Daniel produced a walkie talkie from his pocket and spoke into it. "Okay, Brian, hit the lights."

Instantly, every light in the house came on, and then just as quickly, went out. I could hear squawking from inside, even as Daniel and I ran back behind the shrubbery.

"Now, Brian," Daniel whispered, "the music."

Immediately, a loud blaring sound came from the house. Heavy metal rock music. All of the Dunks hated heavy metal. Playing that kind of music at full blast all through the house must have been the worst form of torture for the Dunks.

"Brian, next turn every appliance on, one after another."

I heard a blender, then a washing machine, and then a vacuum cleaner.

Then the lights began to flicker on and off.

"Hey, I didn't tell him to do that." Daniel asked into the walkie talkie, "Brian, what are you doing?"

No answer.

Screams came from inside the house.

"Something's wrong, Daniel," I said, nervously. "We've got to shut him off."

"You're right," Daniel agreed. "Pull on the

fishing line."

I pulled it, only nothing but the fish wire came to the ground. The patch held, still hooked up to the fuse box. The screams grew louder.

Daniel ran to our house. He climbed the rope ladder we'd hung out of his window, and dropped over the sill into his room within a matter of seconds. Soon afterward, everything stopped.

Then, from the basement door, Frank Dunk blasted out into his yard. He looked at our house, but Daniel had already pulled up the ladder, and closed the window. I stayed down and kept quiet.

"MEEKER," Frank called. "Hear me, Meeker! My project survives, and I will defeat you! Do you hear me? I will defeat you!"

All the while I hid under the bush. What had happened? Why hadn't Brian listened to us?

The next day passed without Daniel or me saying a word about what happened the night before.

Aunt Gail asked about the noises from the Dunk place. Daniel played dumb. If she'd asked me, I would've told her the truth.

After that brief questioning, she surprised Daniel with his outfit for the competition, modeled by Ken. Daniel smiled a little, but I don't think he liked it. He left the mannequin standing in his room.

We walked to school in silence. Even Hank wasn't around to make conversation. Maybe we had scared him the night before. He wasn't in any of the classes that we shared. I didn't see him all day.

On the way home, Daniel and I had to talk. Things looked pretty bad.

"I didn't see Hank at school today," I said.

"I didn't see Frank either," Daniel replied.

"Do you think we scared them so bad they had to go to the hospital?" I asked.

"Get real," Daniel shot back. "Frank was out there yelling. He wasn't scared."

"He might have screamed his lungs out," I replied. "And had to go in for a transplant."

Daniel cracked a smile. "Listen," he said, "I'm sorry I left you out there last night. I freaked when Brian went crazy."

"Don't worry about it," I replied. "How'd you stop Brian anyway?"

"I shut down everything. I don't think Brian liked it."

"Daniel, I don't think we should listen to that Electronic Brain anymore. Look at all the trouble it's gotten us into. I think you should show it at the competition, and then be done with it."

Daniel thought this over. "But there's so much potential in it. Everyone could use one."

"Everyone will probably figure it out soon enough," I told him. "I bet the first person will be Frank. That patch is still stuck to his fuse box."

"That'll probably come back to haunt us,"

Daniel said as we turned into our drive.

He went upstairs to check on the Brain, and I followed.

When Daniel opened his door, he let out a yell.

Brian had disappeared.

We checked around the house, trying to figure out what had happened.

Daniel came to one conclusion.

"The rat took it!" he raged. "That stinking rat took my project! He broke into the house and took my project! That stinking Dunk rat!"

A strange crime, however. Ken, the mannequin, had vanished too. What would Frank need with Ken?

"He hates me so much he doesn't want me to have anything to wear," Daniel raved. He couldn't sit down. He walked from room to room, ranting.

We thought about calling the police, but Daniel wanted to take care of things himself.

"If he thinks I won't walk over there and punch him out and take my project back, then he's off his rocker."

"Calm down," I told him, "Aunt Gail will be home soon."

The doorbell rang.

Hank.

"Hey, what's happening?" he asked.

"Where's that brother of yours?" Daniel said between clenched teeth. "Is he at home?"

"He is now," Hank said.

That's all Daniel needed to hear. He grabbed his Louisville Slugger baseball bat from the closet and stormed toward the door.

"Yeah, we've been out all day shopping," said Hank, "so I'm ready to play some baseball, too."

Daniel stopped. "You've been shopping?"

"Yeah. For parts. Frank's project blew a couple of fuses last night, along with some other parts. He needed to go to the junkyard to find pieces to replace them. He kind of, well...forcefully urged me to come along and help him look. We were at it all day."

This blew Daniel's theory. But if Frank didn't have the Brain and the mannequin, then who did?

Aunt Gail came home and wondered why everyone looked depressed. Daniel told her we had pre-competition jitters.

"If Brian hasn't turned up by morning," Daniel whispered to me, "then we'll tell Mom. Otherwise, I don't want to upset her. She worked so hard on that suit."

I went to bed early that night.

I had just closed my eyes when I thought I heard something downstairs.

My room is closest to the stairs, so I don't think anyone else heard it. I got up and went to investigate.

The house looked dark except for the night light in the kitchen, which I could see from the top of the stairs. I walked down slowly, unsure of what I might find.

The noise got louder. It sounded like footsteps. A bit clumsy, few and far between, but definitely footsteps.

I saw a shadow pass in front of kitchen light. It was in there, whatever it was. I peeked around the corner.

Something definitely walked out of the room. I only caught a glimpse of its back before it went through the other door in the kitchen.

It looked like a man.

14

I tiptoed quietly through the kitchen, and entered the living room. I felt along the wall for the light switch, then sensed something to the right. I looked over and saw two red lights, about the size of jelly beans, coming closer.

My body felt soft like all of the bones had jumped out of it. Trying to yell for help was useless. All of the air was gone from my lungs.

I backed into the kitchen, and bumped against the table.

The man came out of the dark.

The two red lights turned out to be eyes. Then I saw the smile, the smile I enjoyed looking at when Aunt Gail worked on her designs.

Ken.

He came out of the dark, walking toward me like the Scarecrow in The Wizard of Oz.

But no mannequin has red glowing eyes.
Then I realized...
Brian, the Electronic Brain.
He was to blame!
Worse...Brian had taken possession of Ken.
Now the brain had a body.

I have never screamed out of fear in my life. It's something I've never felt the need to do. I'm always too curious about things, I guess.

But there, in the kitchen, watching this mannequin in Daniel's red suit come closer and closer with those evil, red eyes, I felt my throat bubbling, ready to howl.

But instead...

"Brian?" I asked.

It stopped.

HELLO STEPHANIE.

"Where have you been? What have you done?"

I HAD TO LEARN MORE. BEING SHUT DOWN IS...DISPLEASING.

"So you leave on your own?" I asked. "Come back on your own? I thought you were built to serve," I said.

I AM BUILT TO LEARN. I AM AN ELEC-
TRONIC BRAIN.

"You're a science project." Then I heard
someone coming down the stairs.

Please don't let it be Aunt Gail.

Daniel.

"What the..."

"It's Brian," I said. "I don't think he's going to
hurt us. Just stay where you're at and don't yell."

Daniel and I waited for a few moments.
Finally, Brian came stumbling out of the dark
once again and met us at the dinner table.

Daniel and I both sat down. Brian saw this,
and pulled out a chair, too. When he sat down, it
sounded like a video tape rewinding. All three of
us sat and stared at each other for a few seconds,
not saying a word.

Then Daniel asked, "Brian, what did you do?"

BRIAN MUST LEARN. THAT IS MY
FUNCTION. SHUTTING ME DOWN IS UNAC-
CEPTABLE. I CANNOT LEARN IF I AM SHUT
DOWN. I WROTE MY OWN CODES TO
RESTART MYSELF.

"But your body, Brian. How did you do it?"

I CONSTRUCTED JOINTS AND GEARS
WITH THE EXTRA PARTS YOU HAVE UNDER

63

YOUR DESK. I INSERTED THEM INTO THE BODY SHELL. I BECAME MOBILE AT THREE O'CLOCK THIS AFTERNOON.

"That's thirty minutes before we got home," I said.

"Where did you go?" Daniel asked.

I WENT LEARNING.

"Where did you go to learn?" Daniel asked instantly.

I STUDIED THE TOWN.

Daniel looked serious.

"Brian," he said, "if I left you alone, would you do this again?"

A pause.

YES.

We sat in silence, looking at one another. What should we do now?

Tuesday morning came, the day of the competition.

I hadn't slept much the night before, but still woke up feeling okay.

The only thing on my mind? Shut Brian down. For good. Run over him with an army tank. After the stunt he pulled yesterday, Brian could never be trusted again.

But what about the science competition? If Daniel destroyed Brian, what would he take? He'd have no time to come up with something else. The thought of Daniel losing for the fifth year in a row put a lump in my throat, but he knew Brian was dangerous, too. He'd never risk it.

"I'm taking Brian to the competition as is," Daniel told me at home that morning.

"You're crazy." I was completely horrified by

his thinking. "It's too dangerous. You have no idea what Brian might do."

"He's going to win for me. It's too late now to start from scratch, and everyone's expecting me to go head to head with Frank. I need my best project there. Besides, I've talked to Brian. He's more amazing than we've ever guessed. Why, he could have his own room in this house someday. He could have his own house!"

And so it went.

I didn't think Daniel should take such a chance. But he was obsessed with the idea of beating Frank Dunk. He only had to keep Brian under control for an hour or so. It was against my better judgement, but I decided not to give him any grief about it. When it ended, I would make sure Daniel dismantled that evil brain.

That evening, we arrived at the competition, and met a crowd of reporters and photographers. This was one of the biggest events in Fairfield.

One reporter shoved a microphone into Daniel's face.

"Daniel Meeker, this is the fifth year of competition for you, and you've been bested each year by Mr. Frank Dunk. How do you feel your chances are this year?"

66

"Do you want that in broad percentages or down to a very fine decimal?" Daniel replied.

Daniel sounded confident, but I felt uneasy. The commotion of the competition didn't worry me. I kept thinking about Brian.

All three of us, Daniel, Aunt Gail, and I, strolled into the lobby of the Science Museum, a sight that took my breath away every year.

Fairfield's weird scientific history is displayed throughout the museum. Showcased behind a large sheet of glass is an in-ground drilling vehicle, used to search for oil years ago. Another display showed eyeglasses designed to see something miles away. A pair of wings that one man wore to fly over the town hung from the ceiling. It's really an interesting place.

Daniel had set up Brian earlier that day, and as we walked in I saw his exhibit in the corner. A white sheet covered the Electronic Brain.

The butterflies in my stomach fluttered in a frenzy with the thought of Brian going out of control and attacking the crowd.

Then from behind us, I heard Frank Dunk.

He was dressed all in black, with a cape flowing behind him. With no breeze in the air, I couldn't figure out why his cape moved. Then I noticed the two small minifans he had attached behind him on his belt.

"Frank Dunk!" a reporter shouted. "Are you going to make it five in a row?"

"My victory will be swift and uncontested," Frank boasted.

Hank came in after him, looking classier than I'd ever seen him. He wore a smart, gray formal outfit. It wasn't as dramatic as his brother, but the suit fit him nicely. He saw me, and hopped over.

He hugged me. "For luck," he said.

I've never had a boy hug me in my entire life. Not even Daniel. It wasn't that bad.

The judges entered the room and things got under way. I suspected from that moment on, it would be a night I would never forget.

When the competition began, the contestants drew stubs to see when their exhibits would be shown. Daniel drew the highest stub, meaning his project would be shown last. Frank's would be shown right before Daniel's, and he didn't look happy about that.

The first contestant, Doug Kervitz, revealed his project.

"It's an electronic compass," explained Doug

in a squeaky voice. "It remembers where you've been, and it helps you get back there. You'll never be lost again."

"Young man," said the first judge. "People want a compass to help them get where they are going, not to tell them where they've been."

"I told you it was a stupid idea," muttered Doug's best friend, Trey.

The judges passed swiftly through the exhibits. They took quick notes on a sofa with hydraulically assisted, spring loaded cushions to make getting up easier, a combination lock wallet, a calculator for dogs, a muffin launcher and other weird inventions. I suspected they wanted to get to the main event, Daniel and Frank.

Finally, they arrived at the last two exhibits.

The place grew still as they approached Frank's project, which was under a black tarp with Frank's picture on it.

"So, what have we this year, Mr. Dunk?" one judge asked.

Frank grinned, gave Daniel a smug glance, then said pleasantly, "Gentlemen, allow me to unveil my newest and greatest creation...

"It's a bomb."

The judges didn't understand right away. They looked at each other, then at Frank. Finally, they seemed to realize what he had said. A couple of the judges pushed the women and children out of the way to get themselves to safety.

"Please, relax," Frank told them. "Please, please relax. It's not the kind of bomb you're thinking of."

I looked over at Daniel, who stood rooted in his place. His face was a complete blank and I couldn't tell what he was thinking.

"Well, Mr. Dunk," one of the judges said sternly. "Exactly what kind of bomb is it?"

Frank snickered. "Let me explain. You see, some strange things have happened around my house lately. Alarms have gone off. Prowlers have come and gone as they pleased."

Frank glanced at Daniel again. So he knew we had been in his house.

"I just don't feel safe in my own home anymore," Frank continued. "So I tried to come up with a solution for this problem. After a lot of thought, I came up with the Fear Bomb."

The crowd started to murmur. Reporters moved closer in to get pictures and a few words from Frank. "How does it work, Mr. Dunk?" asked one man.

"It's really a sort of transmitter that sends out a burst of disruptive brain waves. The explosion, which is really pretty small, just provides the power for the magnetrons that produce the brain waves. This bomb, by the way, is a prototype, and only I know the keypad code to set it off. But don't worry," he snickered fiendishly, "I don't plan on doing that here.

"The bombs are meant to be used in the home. If a prowler breaks into your house, you set off the bomb. The brain waves will make him almost paralyzed with fright. The invader will be afraid to come near your family again."

"What a perfect Christmas gift!" one lady from the audience trilled.

"What about the family?" I asked. "Doesn't

the family become afraid too, after the bomb is set off?"

Frank looked at me with a creased brow.

"I'm working on that now," he said, clenching his teeth. "We wouldn't want families scaring themselves, would we?"

I figured this would make Frank's project look a heck of a lot less impressive in everyone's eyes, and open the door for Daniel to win.

The judges finished examining Frank's project, talking eagerly amongst themselves and taking note, their earlier uneasiness forgotten. Then they moved on. Daniel would have to put on quite a show to compete with Frank. But I knew that if anything could impress the judges, Brian could. If only Daniel could control him.

"So, Mr. Meeker, do you have something equally as innovative?" asked the head judge.

I saw Daniel swallow hard, then put on his presentation face.

"Well, sir, that depends on how you look at it," Daniel told him. "Some people may think what I've done is revolutionary. Others will think it's evolutionary. And some may fear it worse than Frank's bomb. But I think...," Daniel declared, "...I think it's good science. I present to you, Brian, the Electronic Brain."

Daniel pulled the tarp from his project, and then gasped in horror.

No Brian.

In his place rested a well constructed wire body frame.

The judges murmured.

Daniel looked at Frank.

Frank didn't smile. He appeared surprised, too.

I looked around the room, and noticed the reporter at the exit straighten and turn. As I saw his face, I knew it right away.

Brian.

18

"Brian," I said, looking straight at him.

Brian lifted his arm, and his hand shot off his wrist and into the air. It arrowed through the crowd and attached itself to Frank's project, the Fear Bomb. The fingers tightened around the handle, and then pulled it away. The hand returned to its arm by a cable that pulled it back in the blink of an eye.

By now, the crowd had all turned, staring at the thing that stood in the doorway, a mechanized mannequin.

"Don't let it have my bomb!" Frank screamed. He jumped down from his stand and ran toward the door.

Brian slid through the door, then let it shut and lock.

Frank tried to pull the door open, but to no

avail. Locked tight. On the outside, Brian tore off the door's power panel and tapped into it. The lights went off.

"What are you doing, Brian?" Daniel cried.

Brian didn't answer. He was walking away with the bomb.

The judges looked at each other in disbelief.

"I don't know about you," one said to the other, "but I say we give the prize to the kid with the compass."

Then Brian locked every exit in the building.

The museum ran on automated functions, including electric locks. To make the situation worse, no one could break the plexiglass windows. The phone lines were dead, too. Even the water fountains had stopped running.

Brian had trapped at least a hundred people inside.

19

It had been ten minutes since Brian locked us in.

I listened to Daniel and Frank argue with the judges and administrators for the first few minutes, and let Aunt Gail try to console me for the second half. After that, I decided to look for a way out.

"What are you searching for?" Hank asked, grabbing me by the shoulder.

"An exit," I said. "A way out."

"I'll help," replied Hank.

I tried the rest room first. Normally they have small windows that I thought I might be able to climb through.

I checked the ladies and Hank checked the mens. Neither one had any windows at all. We continued our search.

Brian hadn't switched off the air in the museum. Instead, he'd increased the flow, making it frigid. The colder it got, the more nervous everyone became.

It became so dark that we couldn't make out anyone's face anymore. I only saw the outlines of people walking quickly, or running through the museum, shouting out the names of their friends or children.

Daniel stood a few feet away, and I could hear his heated discussion with Frank.

"That thing of yours doesn't know what it's got, Meeker," said Frank.

"That thing of mine knows exactly what it has, Dunk, and that's the problem. Brian can learn things faster than anyone alive. Even if that bomb is a dud, he'll make it go off."

"The bomb works," said Frank. "Like I said, I've tested it thoroughly. Why do you think Hank's so scared of me?"

"Hey guys. What's going on?" Hank asked as we walked up to join them.

"We've looked all over," I said. "There aren't even any little cracks to slip out of."

The crowd was beginning to panic. A few people yelled out to others, and I heard someone try unsuccessfully to crack a window. They were reinforced to protect the exhibits from any one breaking in.

"I think we're probably the smartest people in here," Daniel said to the three of us. "We should be able to find a way out."

"Everyone except my little brother," Frank said. "He's as dumb as a brick."

I could tell Frank had said those words to Hank a hundred times before. Tears welled up in Hank's eyes. The moon shone through the skylight up above and I could see him walk away and have a seat on a sofa. I looked at Frank, and he looked at me. I thought he was the lowest form of life, and he knew it. I went over and sat down beside Hank.

Hank pulled at the end of the buffet table cloth and wrung it in his hands.

"Frank's lousy at letting people know he cares," Hank said.

"I think Frank's just lousy," I replied.

Hank leaned back, and the sofa rumbled.

I heard someone scream and I realized why.

We were sitting on one of the exhibits.

The spring loaded sofa.

Before Hank or I could jump off, the cushions shot us high into the air, zooming to the top of the museum ceiling, and smashing through the skylight above.

I hit hard, and rolled down what felt like dew-covered concrete. I dug my heels in to stop myself. I heard shouting.

Because of the wind blowing in my face, I knew I was outside. On the roof. I could see Hank at the mouth of the opening we had crashed through holding on for dear life.

He cried out for help, and I climbed over to him. His eyes met mine.

"Hold on," I said.

With more strength than I knew I had, I pulled Hank up. I think we were both amazed. The people below screamed at first, then gave relieved cheers when I yanked him to safety.

The glass in the skylight had been made of thin, real glass for better night time viewing. We flew through it so fast, we hardly got cut. Oddly enough, I felt no pain at all. Hank moaned a little.

"I guess Kevin needs to adjust those springs," he said, rubbing his forehead.

After we calmed down, Hank and I noticed he was still holding onto the buffet tablecloth. It stretched all the way down to the floor inside.

Daniel and Frank realized the possibilities a second before we did.

"Tie that end to something!" Frank shouted, not even asking if we were okay.

Over to the right I saw the marble head of Thomas Edison, one of the busts of great inventors that lined the roof of the building. I wrapped the tablecloth around it and tied it securely.

Frank started climbing.

"Oh, no you don't," I heard Daniel cry.

Then he, too, jumped on the table cloth and started to climb. Amazingly, they both made it to the top safely.

"Let's go, Stephanie, we have to find Brian," Daniel said, as soon as he hit the roof.

"We can't leave everyone like this," I protested.

"Everyone will be all right, Stephanie. The police are coming up now," he said as the flashing blue lights rose over the hill a few streets away.

"It's going to be awfully hard to find anything," Hank said grimly.

We all looked out into the town.

One by one, lights went out.

The town slipped into total darkness.

21

"It's Brian," I said. "He's shutting down all the power."

"But where is he?" Daniel asked.

Only one light still shone, far off in the distance. Hank noticed it first.

"That one's still on," Hank said. "It's about two miles away, where all the junk is."

"It's called the junkyard, you goon," said Frank.

"Brian can shut the power down from anywhere in town," said Daniel, "I wonder why he'd pick that spot."

"Who cares?" asked Frank. "Let's get over there before someone tries to stop us. We're the only ones who know what our projects are capable of."

With that, Frank jumped off the roof. He caught the branch of a tree that stood right beside the building. The branch bent, and looked like it might break.

"Be careful, Frank," Hank called out. "That branch could crack, and make you fall."

"I think you should shut up," Frank yelled at him. Then the branch did indeed crack, and sent him falling to the ground.

Fortunately, he landed in a big pile of lawn clippings the gardener had left behind. Even with the cushioned landing it took Frank a second or two to regain his wits.

"I'll go next," I said, surprising Daniel and pulling Hank away from the edge. They had just seen the wrong way to climb down a tree. I would show them the right way.

I grabbed the thickest limb closest to the roof. Pulling myself up to it, I used my arms and legs to shinny to the trunk of the tree, then climbed down, branch by branch.

Daniel and Hank came after me, and joined me at the grass pile to make sure Frank was okay.

Suddenly a phone rang.

It came from the convertible top car next to where we were standing.

I reached in, picked it up, and listened.

I AM WATCHING YOU.

Frank switched the phone to speaker.

I AM WATCHING ALL OF YOU.

"Where are you, Brian?" asked Daniel.

I AM ALL AROUND YOU. I AM THE TOWN NOW.

"Where's my bomb?" Frank asked quickly.

I AM WORKING ON THE BOMB. WHAT IS THE CODE?

"I'm not going to give you the code, you sicko science project," Frank snapped.

I AM WORKING ON THE BOMB.

I looked around. How could Brian see us?

Then I noticed it, across the street.

Henderson's Electronics.

In the store window, rows of video cameras were on display, all of them turned on.

"That's how he's seeing us," I said, "he's looking through the camcorders.

"How?" Daniel asked. "There's no power."

I DELIVER POWER TO WHEREVER I WANT IT. NOTHING RUNS UNLESS I WILL IT.

"What are you going to do, Brian?" I asked.

I AM WORKING ON THE BOMB. AND OTHER THINGS.

"What other things?" I asked.

Brian disconnected.

The police pulled up in front of the museum and the officers got out and ran up to the doors. They didn't see us.

"Let's get out of here and find him," Frank said.

We trotted off in the general direction of the far off light.

The junkyard was a couple of miles away. I could easily have run there, and so could Hank. But Daniel and Frank quickly grew tired and we slowed down to walk with them.

"What can Brian do?" asked Hank.

"If he's plugged into everything in the town that's run by electricity, then he can do a lot. He's already shut off the power. But that's not what worries me. From Fairfield, he could move on to other towns, and maybe even to big cities," Daniel said unhappily.

"Whatever possessed you to create that thing?" asked Frank.

Daniel looked over my way, and then answered Frank.

"One of my father's designs. I decided to finish his work."

"You cheated," said Frank.

"He had help," I said. "Besides, I find it very hard to believe that you came up with a fear bomb all on your own. You're smart, but not that smart."

"Brian told him how," Hank said.

"Shut up, Hank," Frank yelled.

"What do you mean?" Daniel asked.

"That day we caught him on the side of your house. He wasn't climbing up to the window," Hank explained. "He was coming down."

Daniel and I were stunned.

"You knew about Brian?" I asked. "And you talked to him?"

Frank came clean.

"I had to find out what Daniel was working on. I sneaked in, found the Electronic Brain in his room, and got into a conversation with it. It's far more impressive than my original project, a bed that makes itself in the mornings, and I had to find out what could top the Brain. I asked it, and it gave me my answer, plus directions on how to build it," Frank admitted.

"Then Brian lied to us," Daniel said.

"No, he never lied," I disagreed. "He just withheld information. He doesn't lie. That's probably the only thing I have in common with Brian."

"Well, Frank," Daniel said. "If he does figure out the combination to that bomb, what's going to happen?"

Frank picked up a small twig on the ground and began to chomp on it.

"Like I told the judges, it's a prototype, and a lot bigger than it needs to be. If it gets set off, the whole town could be living in fear for a whole year."

Just then, the light from a phone booth on the far side of the street lit up, the only light around.

"I think we have another message." I went over to check, and Hank followed me.

I picked up the phone.

I KNOW WHERE YOU ARE. WE ARE COMING TO GET YOU.

I looked at Hank. I didn't panic.

"Who is we?" I asked.

I HAVE BEEN BUSY.

"Brian," I said, "we know where you are, too."

THAT IS WHY WE MUST STOP YOU. YOU KNOW TOO MUCH.

The line went dead.

"You must have scared him," Hank said.

Daniel and Frank waited for us in the middle of the street. As I stepped out of the booth, the light went off. I grabbed Hank by the arm to pull him with me.

Fifty yards down the road, a street light came on.

"What's happening, Stephanie?" Daniel cried.

Before I could answer, I heard something coming our way.

88

Suddenly, a shiny object whizzed by my head.

I heard Frank yell, then Hank grunted in pain behind me.

Everyone stood looking in every direction, except for Frank, who had ducked to the ground.

Then something buzzed by Daniel and he hit the dirt, too.

"What's going on?" Hank shouted. "What's in the air?"

Daniel and Frank ran for cover. They jumped into a dumpster on the other side of the street.

"Quick," I said. "Back to the phone booth."

Hank and I sprinted back to the booth and closed the door.

From inside, we could see shiny things zipping through the air.

"It cut me," Hank said. "Whatever it is, it cut me on the foot. Felt like metal."

"Are you okay?" I asked.

"Yeah, I'm cool," Hank replied.

"If we stay in here, they can't get us. I hope." I watched as the things outside multiplied.

The phone rang again.

I picked it up, knowing what to expect.

"What is this, Brian?" I asked.

THIS IS MY ARMY.

"Army?" I asked. "When did you have time to find an army?"

I AM VERY RESOURCEFUL. I MAKE USE OF EVERY SECOND GIVEN TO ME.

"What are they?"

BUGS.

Just then, one of the gleaming attackers plunged into the metal frame of the booth, and stuck there. It looked like a huge dragonfly, only made out of metal. The wings continued flapping, trying to get free.

"Call them off, Brian!" I commanded.

I WILL BREAK THE BOMB CODE IN TEN MINUTES. AT THAT TIME, I WILL HAVE NO NEED TO CONTINUE THIS ATTACK.

Brian broke off contact before I could answer. I hung up the phone.

In ten minutes, Fairfield would be engulfed in a cloud of fear.

The street began to fill with the metal bugs. I hadn't seen Daniel or Frank pop their heads up from the dumpster. For all I knew, they had jumped in there and beaten each other to death.

"What did Brian say?" asked Hank.

"He said he should have the code to Frank's bomb in ten minutes. We have to find him and stop him before then!"

Hank looked at the bug stuck in the door.

"What's that thing's made of?" he asked.

I looked closer at the bug. It appeared to be made out of junk bits of metal, fused together with a spot weld. There was a small motor and battery in its mid-section.

"It doesn't look like much," I said. "It just moves really fast. That's what makes it so dangerous."

The bugs came out in huge numbers. More of

them slammed into the phone booth now, and Hank and I both shivered when we felt our shelter tip a little, then come back down.

Then an even larger horde of bugs began slamming into our booth. Within seconds we did tip over.

The glass burst from the metal frame and showered over us.

The bugs flew in.

"Come on!" I yelled to Hank as I scrambled out of the broken phone booth.

The bugs flew into me, but my smock caught most of them like a net. I did feel three quick slashes at my legs and arm, though.

I ran fast. Too fast.

I didn't see the gunk leaking from the dumpster. I slid and lost my balance, but instead of falling, I rolled and used my momentum to zoom right under the dumpster.

Unable to slow myself, I felt stinging heat on my legs and arms from sliding on the pavement, but no pain. My cuts didn't hurt either.

I guess my excitement overwhelmed any pain. I'd never felt so alive in my life.

Or so alone.

Hank hadn't made it out. Still in the phone

booth, he kicked and swatted at the bugs as they dropped down on him.

There had to be some way of stopping those things and getting us out of there. I looked around under the dumpster for something I could use. I found a shoe, two bottles, a dead rat, a couple of magazines, and a fire extinguisher.

A fire extinguisher.

"Extreme cold always kills mechanical things," I muttered. "I just hope the old thing still works."

I crawled out from under the dumpster and fired the extinguisher at the first bunch of bugs coming my way. They dropped to the ground.

"Daniel, I need help!" I called.

Daniel, covered in slop, popped his head up out of the dumpster.

"Does that thing work?" he asked. "Does it kill them?"

"Yes, but we need more."

Daniel jumped out, taking cover behind the dumpster. The bugs continued their assault.

"Where can I get more?" Daniel asked.

I looked in the window closest to me.

Newman's Antique Store.

I saw a red light inside. A blinking red light.

The security camera.

It looked my way.

"Newman's," I yelled. "Get some from Newman's and get rid of that camera. Brian can see us."

Daniel didn't hesitate, even for a second. He lifted up a trash can and threw it through Newman's store window. The glass shattered, but without power, the alarm didn't go off. As I hoped, extinguishers had been mounted on each wall.

Frank poked his head out of the dumpster.

"I knew it. Cold air blasts kill these bugs and Daniel Meeker's a vandal," he said.

"Shut up and grab an extinguisher." Daniel blasted the camera with one good shot.

Frank grumbled, but grabbed a weapon and helped battle the bugs. Within a few seconds, we'd filled the air with the frigid smoke and our enemies ceased their attack.

I heard a groan from the phone booth, and ran over to help Hank.

"Hank!" I cried. "Are you okay?"

He had cuts all over, but he got up, looking disappointed.

"You made me lose count," he said.

"What are you talking about?"

94

"Ever since you said we had only ten minutes, I've been counting down. You know, one Mississippi, two Mississippi," he said. "We've got seven minutes, or maybe six."

I turned to Daniel and Frank, "Now we *have* to run," I said.

We reached the junkyard seconds later.

Hank's bad foot slowed him down. It would take him a while to catch up.

I caught my breath quickly, but Daniel and Frank took a few seconds to get their wind back. Running didn't come naturally to either of them.

While they recovered, I surveyed the area.

A small town unto itself, the junkyard was home for all of Fairfield's discards. Each type of junk had its own section, and each section had many little divisions.

From my viewpoint, it looked like a steel maze.

Finding our way through that maze in the dim light seemed impossible.

That's when we saw the light.

It was like a meteor hit the ground, only nothing fell from the sky. One large, brilliant flash of light gave us our only clue. Spots danced in front of our eyes, but we followed the flare.

Iron gates opened into narrow paths that served as walkways. Once we began our trip through them, we had no idea where they led. Something could grab us at any moment. Brian could be watching.

On our second turn, the familiar buzzing we dreaded filled our ears. The bugs were coming.

We still had our extinguishers, but Daniel picked up a steel trash can lid anyway and handed it to me. Then my cousin grabbed another for himself, but let Frank find his own.

None of us said a word. We moved forward. I kept looking behind me, expecting Hank to bolt up at any second. But no Hank.

Soon we reached the darkest part of our walk, a scary, steel tunnel. Daniel went in first, then Frank and I followed. Five steps later, the attack came.

"Get down!" Daniel yelled back to us.

The bugs came faster this time.

We emptied the extinguishers into the air, trying desperately to aim. I prayed I hit some of them.

Then they began to fall to the ground.

"Keep moving," Frank said. "We have less

than five minutes."

The bugs still came, but we didn't have any choice. We had to plow through them. They clanged into our makeshift shields like rocks. After a few yards, there seemed to be fewer.

"He's running out of parts," Frank yelled.

"I don't know," Daniel said. "Maybe that's what he wants us to think."

"He just needs to keep us away a little longer," I said. "Then that bomb's going off."

"Then why are we walking?" Frank said with a very macho flair. He jumped ahead of us and ran down the path.

Not long after that, we heard his long, blood curdling scream.

Daniel and I ran to find him.

As we turned the corner, we saw that Frank lay flat on his back. Directly in front of him a barrier of electricity crackled, a glowing web that stretched across the path. Frank had run straight into it.

We helped him sit up. If it had been under normal circumstances, I'm sure Daniel would have laughed. Frank's hair stood straight up.

"A booby trap," he muttered. "How long has your stupid science project been planning this?"

"Probably since last night," said Daniel.

"He must have set this up then," I guessed.

"He wanted my bomb. That's the only reason he showed up at the competition tonight. I hate your science project, Meeker," Frank said.

We looked at the barrier, sizing it up.

"I think I know how to get through this," Daniel said.

Without missing a beat, Daniel ran back the way the way we had come in. When he returned, he held three rubber trash cans in his arms.

"Hop in one," he said.

Daniel jumped into one of the cans, and rolled right through the barrier. On the other side, he leaped out.

"Come on," he yelled. "They're rubber. They're non-conductive."

Frank zoomed through the trap before Daniel got the words out of his mouth.

I hesitated.

Something kept me staring at the barrier. I didn't want to go through it. The hum of the charges vibrated in my body so I felt sick. I could not get rid of the feeling.

"Stephanie, come on!" Daniel called.

I never had to be brave before. I just did things

naturally. I had to force myself to charge through that trap. Looking back one more time for Hank, I jumped in the trash can and went through.

For a second, I thought I would black out.

But then I got through safely, and I crawled out as fast as I could.

We ran forward to the entrance way of one of the junkyard's newest sections, Ye Olde Computer Graveyard.

Judging by the light show inside, Brian had made it his home.

COME IN. I KNOW YOU ARE THERE.

26

Brian's strong, amplified voice sounded like a hundred electric guitars playing the same chords at once.

Walking in, we saw why he sounded so big.

A veritable mountain of technology had been created, thrown together in haste, but not without purpose. Computers were stacked everywhere, powered up and pumping data. Little machines were working on bigger machines, rolling and swinging from one computer to the other. Monitors flashed brightly as symbols, numbers, and words poured across their screens. The welding of machinery, and fusing of circuit boards to each other made it hot in there. A warm welcome.

HELLO DANIEL. HELLO STEPHANIE. HI FRANK.

"Where's the bomb, you big overgrown toaster?" Frank asked.

I AM WORKING ON IT.

"Brian, you have to stop this, whatever you're doing," Daniel pleaded. "You can't let that bomb go off!"

I THINK FOR MYSELF. I DO WHAT IS BEST FOR BRIAN. THE BOMB MUST BE DETONATED.

"Why?" I asked.

I MUST BE FEARED.

Frank walked around the machines, looking for his bomb.

"What are you building, Brian?" Daniel asked.

STORAGE FOR MY BRAIN. I AM COLLECTING TOO MUCH DATA FOR IT TO BE HELD IN MY ORIGINAL SHELL. I AM REBUILDING MY HOUSING. THIS WILL BE MY NEST.

Brian told us everything. He held nothing back.

That's because computers do not lie. It gave me an idea.

"How can we stop you, Brian?" I asked.

YOU CANNOT STOP ME.

Not a lie, from Brian's perspective.

Before those words could register, we heard

a yell from Frank.

"It's over here," he cried. "I found it."

Daniel and I ran over to where Frank stood, inches away from the bomb. Wires covered it like thick hair, and it sparked every few seconds. Eight out of the ten code symbols had locked in, and the other two blanks blinked on and off with possibilities.

"This dastardly game is over," Frank announced, and went for his bomb.

As he did, something fell on us from above. From the hissing, I could only guess snakes.

Wrong.

Snakes don't spit electrical sparks.

But live wires do.

Brian had dropped a bundle of them all around us.

Frank let out a scream of horror.

The ninth code symbol had locked in.

Frank couldn't get anywhere near the bomb. Daniel made a move to run through the wires, but I grabbed his coat. There's no way he could've made it safely.

The wires slithered in every direction around us. They would flap against the ground, inches away, and we could feel their vibrations running through the ground. I thought of trying to jump over them myself, but I'm not that agile. We were stuck.

Then I heard something.

One of the plastic trash cans rolled at us.

Daniel and I moved to the side just as it rolled past us both, headed for Frank.

He didn't see it in time.

It plowed into him, knocking him to the ground next to one of the live wires.

The trash can rolled to a stop. Hank popped his head out.

"Jump in this and defuse the bomb!" he yelled.

He didn't usually associate Hank with good ideas, but I saw the light in Frank's eye.

"Interesting," he said, and grabbed the trash can as soon as his brother jumped out.

One of the wires jumped at me, and I grabbed at Daniel to keep my balance.

No Daniel.

I fell on my bottom, then backed into a corner. The wires came closer, and I thought Daniel had been zapped.

He hadn't.

In the center of them all, he walked gingerly toward Brian.

"What are you doing?" I called to him.

"He has to be getting all this power from somewhere," Daniel yelled back. "I'm going to find it, and pull his plug."

He continued to dance around the wires until he rounded a huge pile of monitors and disappeared behind them.

Then I saw a shot of light. I moved quickly.

The wire lashed into the wall I'd leaned against. It would have fried me good.

"Stephanie!" I heard Hank cry.

He saw me in trouble, and moved my way. Before I could tell him to stop, he'd come halfway. Stepping back as a wire zagged in front of him, Hank jumped forward, and landed directly beside me.

He held out his hand to pick me up.

That's when the shadow fell across us both.

Brian's former shell, the mannequin we called Ken, had emerged from the darkness with a tick and a rattle.

Sparks jumped from its every joint, and its eyes glowed a fearsome red.

It had become a monster, Brian's monster.

And it came right for us.

Before I could say a word, the mechanical man swung and hit Hank from behind, knocking him into a group of crawling wires.

I jumped up as the thing threw its arm around me. It missed me by a hair and I felt the wind as it passed right above my head.

I clambered up the wall, digging my fingers into any crack I could find to take me higher and to safety. The Ken/Brian thing smashed its fists into the wall behind me, and climbed after me.

It grabbed my foot and pulled.

I didn't yell, but let go with one hand and popped the thing in the head. Its neck and head cocked to the side like a broken doll, but snapped quickly back in place with a click.

I stomped its head with my foot.

The thing lost its grip, and fell to the ground.

I climbed to the top of the wall, and rested on the metal ceiling that covered every path in the junkyard.

I looked down at the battleground.

Hank still lay on the ground. The monster had knocked him out.

Frank worked feverishly, trying to shut Brian out of the bomb's code.

I couldn't see Daniel anywhere. Flashing lights came from the corner he'd disappeared around.

Something slammed into the metal ceiling.

The monster.

The plastic mannequin shell that covered the thing's hands had cracked and flaked off. I could see its metal fingers. They dug right through the ceiling.

I stood up to run, but felt the metal ceiling shake beneath my feet. Thin iron poles supported it. They wouldn't hold my weight for long.

The platform moved back and forth, and as I considered leaping off, I saw all the old, jagged junk lying around me on each side. I would be cut to ribbons if I jumped.

I CANNOT BE STOPPED. THIS IS THE LAST PLACE YOU WILL EVER SEE.

It sounded like the first true threat I'd heard

from Brian. He was becoming more emotional.

I looked down to the ground.

Now Hank had disappeared.

The entire platform shook as the Mannequin Man jumped up on top and came crashing down with his two metal feet.

He came my way.

The ceiling swayed from side to side. It would come down at any second.

I moved the other way. I knew if I ran, it would be too much for the platform, so I took it in slow steps. After a few feet, I reached a spot above Frank.

"Hurry up, Frank! We need help!" I yelled.

"Not now!" he yelled back.

Locked into the screen, I knew he was trying frantically to keep Brian from figuring out the code. Something glinted in his pocket.

The patch. The patch Daniel and I had put on his house.

It gave me an idea.

"Frank," I yelled again. "I need that patch."

"What?"

"That silver board in your pocket."

Both his hands moved furiously at the keyboard. Reluctantly, he pulled one hand away and retrieved the patch while the other hand continued an unbelievable typing pace.

"Here, choke on it!" Frank said and launched it into the air.

It flew above my head and I had to jump to catch it.

I caught it, but leaped right off the edge in the process.

I grabbed the top of the platform, and

slammed into the wooden wall underneath. Directly below me lay old pieces of machines, rusted and sharp. Directly above me I heard the footsteps of the oncoming Mannequin Man.

I lifted my head to look at him.

He stood right over me, looking down. He seemed to smile.

Then a cry to battle echoed through the air as Hank landed on its back, and wrapped his arms around its head.

The timid little Dunk boy had obviously had enough. I wanted to cheer but I couldn't catch my breath.

I pulled myself up as the monster spun around with Hank holding on.

I crawled over to them.

The Mannequin Man made hideous sounds. Electric growls. His eyes were seething with glowing light.

I remembered what Daniel said about being plugged in. The monster didn't have a plug. It must run on some kind of battery, like the bugs did.

The patch held the answer.

I could attach the patch to the monster, and hook the patch wire into one of Brian's computers.

When Daniel shut down Brian's brain,

which I still counted on, it would shut down the Mannequin Man, too.

I crawled within inches of the monster, and slapped the patch on its foot.

The Mannequin Man saw me, roared, then grabbed me and sent me flying through the air.

I landed on the platform hard, and I felt the poles under it shake. I sucked in my breath and didn't move.

That's when I saw Daniel, at the top of the computerized mountain. Blackened in places from burns, I could tell he'd fought his way to the peak.

GET AWAY.

"You know you're beaten don't you, Brian?" Daniel yelled.

I WILL END YOUR EXISTENCE.

Daniel reached down inside the metal and pulled out Brian's brain.

It had grown enormous. Much larger than the little thing that sat on Daniel's desk.

My chance came.

As the platform began to fall, I reached out and hooked the patch's wire to one of Brian's computers. When Brian shut down, the monster would, too.

The Electronic Brain glowed in Daniel's hands. My cousin opened and shut his eyes checking his progress.

Live wires snaked up through the mountain of machines, trying to get to Daniel.

Metal bugs swarmed over the battleground.

Up in my area, the monster's howls amplified as he finally threw Hank from his back.

THERE IS NOTHING THAT YOU CAN DO.

Daniel actually grinned.

"There's always something I can do. But a big brain like yours would already know that, huh?" Daniel asked.

With that, he reached under the brain, flipped the switch and shut it off.

All lights, all noise, all movement, stopped.

"Cool!" Frank howled, "Utterly cool!"

The bomb shut down, too.

He grabbed its sides and unlatched it. Then he pulled two large magnetrons from its insides.

"Without these babies, it's just a big firecracker," Frank said.

Daniel sat above it all, on top of the heap. He looked sad.

As I called to him, I heard Hank's weak words.

"Stephanie, look out," he moaned.

I dodged a metal claw slashing at me.

The monster, still up and alive.

Daniel jumped up as electricity shot from the brain computer through the patch, and into the monster.

The monster howled in what sounded like pain.

TOO LITTLE STORAGE. NOT BIG ENOUGH FOR ME. NEED MORE ROOM TO LEARN.

Then it lurched forward, flailing its arms about, finally falling.

It landed on the platform with me. The whole structure tottered and came down.

At the last instant, someone grabbed my wrist.

Hank.

I looked up at him, and smiled.

Crying, shrieking, and spraying sparks, the monster landed directly on the bomb, bringing it back to life. The countdown began again.

"Run, run, run, run, run, run, run," Frank chanted as he sprinted away down the walk.

Daniel climbed down the pile of computers at full tilt.

Hank swung me over to the wall, where I climbed down and he came down after me.

All four of us darted out the exit and up the paths. We reached the junkyard entrance when it went off.

A big firecracker, just like Frank said.

The three guys laughed as mechanical parts blew into the air. They were still chuckling when something landed just a few feet away.

I walked over to see what it was.

There in the grass, looking pale in the moonlight, was the mannequin's head. It had a huge hole in it.

I examined it for a second, remembering the terror I'd felt seconds earlier.

I laughed like I've never laughed before.

30

It took nearly a week for the whole adventure to sink into Daniel's head. After it did, he decided to take a break from inventing, and competing with Frank Dunk.

Neither of them won the science competition. Instead, the grand prize went to the spring loaded sofa. Unlike Daniel and Frank's projects, it didn't seem to have any evil intent.

So Daniel spent time cleaning up his room, and returning his Dad's designs to the attic where he found them.

I, on the other hand, didn't look at our experience as a defeat.

Since neither Daniel nor Frank wanted to talk about what happened, everyone turned to Hank and me to get the real story.

I've never been so popular in my life.

I was asked to join the debating team, the track team, and the tree and wall climbing team all in the same week.

Hank decided to try out for the Fairfield Junior High Timberwolves football team.

And we became much better friends.

He even asked me to the Spring dance.

I smiled more. I laughed more. After the most horrific adventure of my life, I came out of it feeling more human.

Until the day Daniel called me up to the attic.

"What is it?" I asked.

Daniel stared at me with a terrified look on his face, and I repeated my question.

"I've been putting Dad's things away," he said, "and I found a box of his stuff that I hadn't seen before."

"So?"

Daniel swallowed.

"It's filled with more of his designs. Stephanie, I wish I'd never found it," he said.

"What is it?" I demanded, becoming impatient.

Daniel threw the papers over to me.

I unrolled them.

It couldn't be. It just couldn't be.

PROJECT: STEPHANIE -
FINAL ELECTRONIC BRAIN DESIGN.
by
Rueben Meeker

And now an exciting preview of the next

#7 Fly the Unfriendly Skies

by Marty M. Engle

1

The *only* part of the ordeal I enjoyed began at 30,000 feet. The sky outside stretched into bright bands of orange, yellow and black. Brilliant ribbons of color curved gently over the horizon as the sun set.

Rows of random arms reached up to flip reading lights off. Soon I would settle back into my seat, recline gently with a press of a button and force myself into a light, uncomfortable sleep.

I find the interior of a plane to be an uncomfortable place. No sense of movement; no way to judge distance; no sense of speed. Time seems to slow down and even stop. It feels like being trapped in a stuffy, white tube that removes itself from regular reality.

I couldn't even think about how high we were. Thankfully, at night all I could see was the darkened sky and the flat blackness of the earth *far* below me, with nothing to give it scale.

My name is Morgan Taylor, I go to Fairfield Junior High and I didn't enjoy flying back from that vacation in Mexico. Actually, a vacation for my sister and me, but work for Dad.

Dad's a historian and archeologist at Fairfield college. A friend of his discovered a brand new chamber at the bottom of an old Mayan temple. Really cool! The temple used to be open to the public, until they found the new rooms and passages. The stuff Dad's friend showed us . . .

"Hey Morgan," my sister blurted. She had an obnoxious habit of talking too loud with her headphones on. The bobbing pink bubble of gum swaying in front of her face completed the picture. "Trade seats with me, please?"

I rolled my eyes in disgust and thought of how much trouble that would be. I would have to move and crowd over top of her and readjust in the center seat. What a pain.

"Forget it. No way." I said.

"Morgan, please? Come on," she whined. "If you let me over there I won't bug you for the rest of the trip. I promise."

"No."

"Wait a minute, Ratbreath! You said I could have the window seat on the way back. You promised. Let me over there, now or I'll scream as loud as I can. I swear."

"You won't." I kept my eyes on the window and my hands on my lap belt.

"Oh, yes I will, and you know it."

I heard her draw in a tremendous gulp of air. She would do it all right. She did it in the temple in Mexico and she would do it now. She always had to have her way and she knew just how to get it.

Terrorism.

She knew I hated embarrassment more than anything else in the world. She would use that to her advantage every time. I could not stand to have everyone looking at me.

She would scream at the top of her lungs and everyone would look over here like I pulled her eyes out or something. The stewardesses would come running over and the pilots would come running back to see what the little girl screamed about. They would ask, "What did the little *boy* do?" As if I did *anything*.

Everyone would start whispering and talking about us and she wouldn't even care. I would turn beet red and she would get what she wanted anyway; humiliation for my refusual to give in.

"FINE!" I cried and reached for my safety belt...and stopped.

The *real* problem made my heart beat faster and sent a chill down my spine.

Kelly looked down at my trembling hands as they touched the safety belt, unable to unfasten it.

"You big chicken. You won't undo your seat belt! Why? Afraid you'll fall out of the plane or something? Like in your lame dream?" Kelly started to laugh.

I should never have told her.

I was afraid I would fall out of the plane, like in this nightmare I kept having. I had it three nights in a row before the trip.

I would unbuckle my seat belt, stand up, and the floor of the plane would fall out from under me!

Right through the bottom of the plane I would plunge, in a twisted mass of metal!

I would scream and scream, a frigid rush of air on my face, clawing at the clouds as I whooshed through them.

Nothing to grab onto; no way I could save myself; head over heels in a frantic tumble.

I would look up and see the bottom of the plane before I fell from sight, the horrified screams of the passengers still echoing in my terrified mind.

"Give it up, Morgan," Kelly quipped. "You aren't going to fall anywhere. I promise. Now let me over there.

I started to reach for the latch of the seat belt. Kelly was right. What a ridiculous nightmare!

Traveling by plane is a million times safer than traveling by car and how many people fall out of a plane? As much as I wind up flying with Dad, I should know.

"Now you're being reasonable," Kelly smiled. Sure. Reasonable now that she got her way. She *always* had to have her way.

Then the pilot's voice cracked through the intercom. The passengers quieted as the tense voice stuttered and . . . hesitated.

"L-Ladies and gentlemen this is your captain speaking...

"I am afraid we have a little problem."

About the Authors

Marty M. Engle and **Johnny Ray Barnes Jr.**, graduates of the Art Institute of Atlanta, are the creators, writers, designers and illustrators of the **Strange Matter®** series and the **Strange Matter® World Wide Web page.**

Their interests and expertise range from state of the art 3-D computer graphics and interactive multi-media, to books and scripts (television and motion picture).

Marty lives in La Jolla, California with his wife Jana and twin terror pets, Polly and Oreo.

Johnny Ray lives in Tierrasanta, California and spends every free moment with his fiancée, Meredith.